GOOD
SHOW

GOOD SHOW

Phylliss Adams
Eleanore Hartson
Mark Taylor

Illustrated by John Sandford

MODERN CURRICULUM PRESS
CLEVELAND · TORONTO

ISBN 0-8136-5403-3 (Hardbound)
ISBN 0-8136-5903-5 (Paperback)   123456789   92   91

"Thank you," said Cora Cow.
"That was a good ride."

"I am Ditto," said a man.
"I have a good magic show."

"Oh, I love magic shows," said Cora.

"Come and see my show,"
Ditto said.
"You will like what you see."

"Now I have to get the things
for my show," said Ditto.
"Do you have things to get?"

"Yes," said Cora.
"I will get my things.
Then I will go with you
to see your show."

"We will find our things here,"
said Ditto.

"Look at all the things come out,"
said Cora.

"And they come out so fast,"
said Ditto.

"Oh, this is bad," said Cora.

"Yes, it is," said Ditto.
"I can not find the things
for my show."

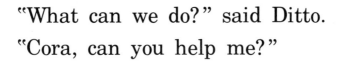

"What can we do?" said Ditto.
"Cora, can you help me?"

"Yes, I can," said Cora.
"Cora to the rescue!"

"We will work fast," said Cora.
"Blue things go on this side.
Red things go on that side.
And green things go on
that little truck."

"This is good," said Cora.
"Now we can get things
one at a time."

17

"Cora, that was a big help,"
said Ditto.
"Now I can help, too.
I will do my magic show here."

"Look at Ditto," said Cora.
"What a show!"

"Thank you, Ditto," said a man.
"That was a good show."

"And that was a good rescue, Cora,"
said a girl.

"We all love you, Cora," said Ditto.
"This is for you."

"Thank you," said Cora.
"I love a good show.
And I love a good rescue!"

Show Time

If necessary, read these directions to the child:
Read each word.
Then find what the word names.

dog

cookie

bed

top

fan

mouse

Help! Help!

Stop my truck.
Help me pick up my things.
Can you find my shoe?
Can you show me the way out?

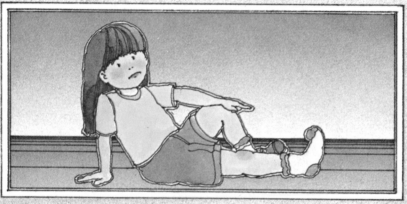

Read each sentence.
Then find the person who asked for help.

No Show

clown   tiger

balloons   flowers

Tell what is missing in each picture.
Then find the word that names it.

trucks   puppets

girls   balls

All the words that appear in the story *Good Show* are listed here.

a	get	not	thank
all	girl	now	that
am	go		the
and	good	oh	then
at	green	on	they
		one	things
bad	have	our	this
big	help	out	time
blue	here		to
		red	
can	I	rescue	too
come	is	ride	truck
Cora Cow	it		
		said	was
Ditto	like	see	we
do	little	show	what
	look	side	will
fast	love	so	with
find			work
for	magic		
	man		yes
	me		you
	my		your

About the Authors

Phylliss Adams, Eleanore Hartson, and Mark Taylor have a combined background that includes writing books for children and teachers, teaching at the elementary and university levels, and working in the areas of curriculum development, reading instruction and research, teacher training, parent education, and library and media services.

About the Illustrator

Since attending the American Academy of Art in Chicago, Illinois, John Sandford has concentrated on illustration for books and magazines.

The artist works in Chicago, where he lives with his wife, Frances. The illustrations for Cora Cow were executed in the spirit of the artist's father, who left to the Sandford family the rich legacy of his creativity.